FORGO̶T̶T̶E̶N̶ BLOOD

INDIAN SOLDIERS IN EUROPE WORLD WAR 1

KAMALJIT S. SOOD

UNION BRIDGE BOOKS
An imprint of Wimbledon Publishing Company Limited (WPC)

UNION BRIDGE BOOKS
75–76 Blackfriars Road
London SE1 8HA

www.unionbridgebooks.com

First published in the UK and USA by Anthem Press 2020

A CIP record for this book is available from the British Library.

ISBN-13: 978-1-78527-323-0 (Pbk)
ISBN-10: 1-78527-323-X (Pbk)

This title is also available as an e-book.

PRELUDE TO THE PLAY

LAHORE – capital of the Pakistani province of Punjab. Country's second most populous city after Karachi.

The play is based on the author's convictions on the social and, to some extent, the socio-political situation in India with respect to the Raj at the outbreak of the First World War. The author has studied extensively the period through readings and by talking to people with family connections of one generation to the 1914 period. I believe that my understanding of the social and sociopolitical situation is largely accurate – that at the beginning of 1914, Punjab was strongly in the grip of Britain as a colonial power, and that the inhabitants of Punjab were largely satisfied with the growing wealth that they were producing every year and that this satisfaction was as a result of the policies of infrastructure development pursued by the British administration. The British administration had brought about an era of social peace and this had benefited the local population. Further, by providing the benefits of military recruitment, it ensured further economic benefits to the various classes that the rulers chose to promote – all with the aim of securing the Raj.

Despite these social benefits, politically, it offended some sections of the population, mainly the intelligentsia, some of whom took up the cause of self-rule, although not independence, and some of whom called for the overthrow of colonial rule through revolutionary and other means. The authorities responded to these activities with a repressive and iron-fist approach, an approach that was perhaps the traditional way of controlling the ruled people of almost every country at the time. But the level of repression was quite alien to the approach taken against their own citizens in England who held similar views both in regard to the conditions in England and in India.

When the war broke out in 1914, India was called upon to provide the manpower. India and Indians rose to the occasion selflessly and provided the needed manpower for use in Europe, the Middle East and East Africa. This manpower provided the strong backbone needed to defend the crown possessions and indeed to stall the advance of the Germans in France and defeat the Germans in East Africa and the Middle East. The Indian forces provided both fighting manpower and auxiliary manpower – the latter was many times more than the former.

This play is written about the evolution of the sociopolitical scene from 1914 until 1919, until just after the event of the Jallianwala Bagh massacre. The author believes firmly that the enthusiasm and willingness with which India responded at the time to the need of the hour in Britain, needs to be appreciated much more in a militarily comradely way, by the main benefactors of these sacrifices, that is the French and the British people and the British establishment, which encompasses the Crown and the government, the than just in forgotten histories, or even in histories that are not fully forgotten. The appreciation needs to remain alive for ages.

The evolution of the sentiments, lifestyles, and values is highlighted through the experiences of two very close Indian friends from school onwards into the battle space in Europe and the death of one and the return of the other to India. It explores with some glimpses of the lifestyle and the family and social values and links it to the values of duty. This gives some insight into the driving force behind the unquestioned way the Indian went to the battlefields in Europe wholeheartedly. These two are imagined characters. But it depicts the psyche of an Indian family life that governed the youth and families in general at the time, the psyche that was common in India in 1914 – almost favourable acceptance of British rule.

1. Great grandson of Guddu and Lucy return to Lahore in 2017. Gudd travels with his girlfriend. They visit the village of his great grandfather's best friend, Jassi. He promised his great grandfather that one day he would return to India on his behalf and finally say goodbye to his best friend.
2. Party for graduating best friends – Jassi / Guddu. Positive about the future.
3. Jassi tells his best friend that he is nervous about joining the military. Guddu tells him that he's being foolish and a coward and that he should think about the debt of gratitude that he owes to the family tradition of military service to which his father belongs. Jassi tries to explain that perhaps on the surface his father is strong and funny and popular but with his own son he is a martinet and gives the feeling of being uncaring.
4. Guddi and Jassi talk. She is anti-war and anti-imperial rule and Jassi respects what she has to say. She convinces him to not to join the Army.
5. Jassi tells his father he doesn't want to join Guddu in continuing in the Army. There is a massive argument. The biggest argument to date. Jassi mentions the fact that he has spoken to Guddi and that she makes some really good points. Jaspreet is furious that his son is listening to such disrespectful nonsense. Eventually, Jassi is worn down by his father's emotional bullying and decides to join the Army.
6. Jaspreet and Gurnam have a FALLOUT. The first time they have ever argued over anything. Perhaps here we get the India versus Britain argument?
7. Guddu and Jassi join the Army and are stationed in France to fight for the Allied Forces.
8. A going away party where the families drop their differences and choose to celebrate their respective sons' immediate futures. There is tension when Guddi appears because she is

still very anti-war. Guddu makes a promise that on his return from the battlefield he will marry Rani.

9. The battlefields of France. The two friends are separated. There is shock, fear and terror. NOW IN THE PLAY THERE IS THE MOMENT IN THE HOUSE IN FRANCE.

10. Brighton – Guddu is in hospital – bad injuries – he meets Lucy. He is informed of Jassi's death. Killed while trying to save the life of another. Guddu is devastated. He is comforted by Lucy and over time during his convalescence they fall in love. He has a dilemma. He has promised to marry Rani but is in love with Lucy. The lack of communication with home alienates Guddu somewhat from the family and his father comes to see him at Brighton. He finds that Guddu is in love with Lucy. He is devasted somewhat but acquiesces to the situation. When he gets home, he tells Jaspreet to find another match for Rani. Rani is devasted but decides to live with her fate.

11. They go to India but Jallianwala Bagh upsets both of them – Lucy very strongly – and Lucy convinces Guddu to go to England where they will be better able to seek redress and justice, both in law and in peoples' minds and attitude.

12. Guddu regrets for the rest of his life the passing away of Jassi due to battlefield injuries. Never saying goodbye to his best friend.

13. Great grandson of Guddu and Lucy return to Lahore in 2017. He travels with his girlfriend. They visit the remembrance grave of his great grandfather's best friend, Jassi. A promise fulfilled, but with renewed vigor emotionally that his ancestors paid a severe price through sacrifice and that sacrifice needs to be remembered in a somewhat glorified way.

The two families have always wanted their children to marry – the sons marrying the daughters.

Jassi has always liked Guddi but Guddi has other ideas.

CHARACTERS – SIKHS

PAMMI – Great grandson of Guddu – got a first at Oxford PPE and went on to do PhD in history at Balliol College Oxford – access to the best education in UK – immersed in free speech and thought – believes that we should live in the world as a nation with the best values of life –experience of and exposure to British values through press and education has shaped him.

LILY – Age about 21, in 2017, Oxford-educated, PPE with a first. Met Pammi at Oxford Union and their love affair blossomed. Lily has some Indian roots. She has linkages to Vivien Leigh family, love for India. She is an idealist and this is one cause of attraction to Pammi.

LUCY – About 21 of age when she was widowed – went to India in 1913 – found a husband in the British army in India who died in India at one of the early frontier wars.

GUDDU – A master's degree with the matric qualification from Aitchison college and masters from Forman Christian College in March 1914. About 23 years of age, son of GURNAM, a very respected lawyer in Lahore with strong connections to the upper reaches of the government. Known for his liberal views and fearless challenges to the government but, nevertheless, accepted by the establishment as their man.

GUDDI – Guddu's sister, about 21 years of age in 1914 with a law degree from Forman Christian College, schooled at Convent of Jesus and Mary; even more progressive than her father, strong views on what may today be considered as human rights. Very concerned about government high handedness and oppressive actions against free-thinking liberals who espouse more freedom and opposition to British Rule.

JASSI – Guddu's inseparable mate from childhood, Masters degree with the matric qualification from Aitchison college and masters Forman Christian College in March 1914. At the same time as Guddu, son of JASPREET – a senior officer in British Indian Army, having a "soldierly" control in the running of his family as well. Well respected in his family, but sometimes imposes his will on matters relating in particular to what he sees as family tradition and honor.

RANI – Jassi's sister, traditional girl, graduated from the Convent of Jesus and Mary, tradition-loving girl, marriageable age.

Pammi and Pammi's girlfriend, Lily, return to Lahore in 2018. They visit the military remembrance of his great grandfather's best friend, Jassi. Pammi promised his great grandfather that one day he would return to India on his behalf and finally say goodbye to his best friend.

ACT 1

SCENE 1

In the taxi, after alighting at Amritsar station, driving — getting close to the war memorial.

IN TAXI

Silence for a while.

Lily: What are you thinking Pammi? As you look out of the window?

Pammi: I don't know.

Lily: What are you feeling? You've been silent since we got off the train.

Pammi: I don't know what to say.

Lily: Your great grandfather would be proud.

Pammi: Hmmmmmmmmmm?...................

Taxi Driver: The book. What is the book you're holding so dear to you?

Pammi: My great grandfather wrote a sort of memoir. For me. Something for me to remember him by.

Beat.

Taxi Driver: You are from UK?

Lily: London.

Pammi: But my family is originally from Lahore ... this is my first visit to the country of my ancestors.

Taxi Driver: I see.

Pammi: My grandfather told me many stories that were told to him by my great grandfather.

Taxi Driver: Did he tell you the story of Jallianwala Bagh?

Pammi: Yes. Many times.

Taxi Driver: The British LIKE TO forget this.

Pammi:	My great grandfather never forgot it. He was an almost direct witness to the tragedy.
Taxi Driver:	Indians will never forget.
Pammi:	My great grandfather lost his best friend in the war in 1914. They were both fighting in France. For Britain. His friend lost his life.
Taxi Driver:	So many friends lost their lives.
Pammi:	Sure. My great grandfather called Guddu lost his *langotia* friend (*childhood dear friend*) Jassi. He felt so sad at his death, that he would forever remember him at every chance he got. Jassi, to my grandad, was such a physically and mentally talented person. Guddu could not forgive himself, he used to reminisce, because Guddu forced Jassi to join the army for the war effort, against the values that had evolved in him. And he did so only because he was like his twin to him. He used to reminisce many moving stories about the war and the sacrifice. I wanted to bring my grandad here though he was frail. But he passed away about three years ago. I cannot forgive myself for that miss.
Lily:	Which is why we're going to the memorial first. To pay our respects.
Pammi:	To finally pay my great grandfathers our respects.

Beat.

Taxi pulls up at the memorial.

Taxi Driver:	Here we are.

Silence.

Lily:	Okay?
Pammi:	I think so.
Taxi Driver:	Take your time. I will wait for you.
Lily:	Thank you.

Sound of car doors opening.

(*They visit the memorial and place the garland of flowers at the foot of the memorial together with a specially handcrafted card with the following words Pammi reading from the memorial?*:

IN LOVING MEMORY OF MY FELLOW COMMUNITY WHO SELFLESSLY GAVE AWAY THEIR LIVES FOR THE BRITISH CROWN. Then, at the memorial, he says a few words.)

Pammi: I cannot but think that even you too are my great grandfather, Jassiji. This memorial is a homage both to the dead soldiers and soldiers like you who were killed during the 1914 war. Let this visit be a homage from both my great grandpa and from my family and our special love for you. Gudduji reminisced so much about you. I wish I could have replicated that friendship that you had with Gudduji. GUDDU TOLD ME SO MUCH ABOUT YOU AND WHAT YOU USED TO GET UP TO. THAT you were together all day long for your life here, at school, at cricket, at Kabaddi, at Polo – name what you wish. And at the most glamorous of all – *Heera Mandi* – the nightlife of choice of the elite professionals who relished the *tawaifs* and cultural figures alike. And do you remember the early morning bicycle rides that you used to go with Gudduji, picking up damsels on the top floor terraces and passing on your beautiful couplets to them, and flirting with young women who had gone out to fetch water from the wells? And what about the fun events that you participated in like Holi, Lohri, Vaisakhi, where no beauty could pass you without being commented in poetic couplets appreciating their beauty, their bodily curves and their moves. And even the simplest young girl, on hearing your couplets, felt her beauty to be beyond this world? And do you remember the way they grimaced (internally very approving but overtly showing their displeasure) at you as if you were rogues. And then getting a dressing down from your fathers for being "disrespectful" of women (though we later learnt that they felt happy that their sons were becoming real men). You were great friends, tied in heart, mind and spirit and full of altruism for each other and others, the likes of which I have not seen anywhere either in real life or literature. He loved you Jassiji. And I am honoured finally to come over here to pay my respects to that wonderful story of you both.

I wish, I wish, I wish that such a story could be repeated.
I hope and pray that your spirit is listening to all this and
responding to me. I can hear the vibes.

(Pammi wipes some tears)

Lily: *(Hugs Pammi sharing his emotions)* Your words make me so proud.

Pammi: They were just young boys then, our age, weren't they?

Lily: All of them, and so many of them, were all boys with the best
of their lives ahead of them.

Pammi: I cannot even say Goodbye Jassiji. But I am constrained. I have
to say that and move on.

(Pammi and Lily, hand in hand, start to walk back)

Lily: Do you feel relieved now? After longing for this for so long
in England?

Pammi: "Relieved" is an understatement. Gudduji's inner feelings will
always be part of me. This is what I am.

(They get into the taxi. It is still early afternoon.)

Taxi Driver: You have made your great grandad very proud today.

Pammi: *(to Taxi Driver)* Can we go see Jallianwala Bagh *NOW*?

Taxi Driver: The place where the British turned their guns to massacre our
women and children and our elders?

Pammi: I need to see this place for myself. I too need reminding of that
fateful day.

Taxi Driver: Get in. I will take you now.

They get into the taxi. Some music on the car radio. This music cross-fades into 1914.

Pammi: It was a very dark day of what can now be called our
shared history.

Pammi: (V/O) The music. I remember the music playing. Jassi and I
stood outside of the party about to start the rest of our lives.
The music was wonderful.

ACT 2

SCENE 1

Music fades in. Back to 1914 Guddu and JASSI GRADUATE FROM FORMAN
CHRISTIAN COLLEGE WITH A MASTER'S DEGREE – AND THEY HAVE
COMPLETED THEIR ARMY OFFICER'S TRAINING PART 1 AND ARE READY TO
RECEIVE COMMISSION

Jassi starts a discussion about his future.

Guddu: Feel proud to receive this master's degree certificate.

Jassi: Supposed to be the highest level of education in the land from the best college. Aren't we privileged? We can feel a bit special.

Jassi is in a contemplative mood

Guddu: What's wrong?

Jassi: Nothing.

Guddu: So why so quiet?

Jassi: I'm not.

Guddu: Three months after college that followed our six months of training while at college has landed us in a position of getting a commission. Not bad, isn't it? But you haven't said a word since we got off the train. This is the time for celebration. You walk around like the world is upon your shoulders.

Jassi: How long have we known each other?

Guddu: Since the moment we started breathing.

Jassi: All our lives.

Guddu: More. We probably knew each other while we were in our mums' wombs!!!!! Our mothers were so close together while we were still in their bellies.

Jassi: Even though they did not know our sex while we were in their bellies!

Guddu:	But it turned out this way and that made their pre-birth talk meaningful.
Jassi:	And we have done everything together.
Guddu:	As best of … best of … best of … friends should.
Jassi:	You are my best friend in the world Guddu.
Guddu:	And you to me. Now what is your problem?
Jassi:	No problem. Post-degree reflection only.
Guddu:	Good.
Jassi:	I am having doubts about joining the army.
Guddu:	What? Did I hear you correctly? This is a bombshell for me.
Jassi:	I am having doubts about joining the army.
Guddu:	What doubts?
Jassi:	Doubts.
Guddu:	You're making no sense to me.
Jassi:	I don't know whether this is what I want. I mean joining the armed forces.
Guddu:	Of course this is what you need to do, at this time at least. The Army is in your family blood.
Jassi:	So?
Guddu:	You cannot abandon at a whim? You have a family tradition to respect.
Jassi:	At home, I am constantly being reminded by my dad about the necessity of following the family line and joining the army.
Guddu:	And because we are one, I too have chosen the army life. I knew that you had a strong family tradition to honour and the only way for me to be near you was to go to the army with you. At least we will be together. Meet very often. And it is adventurous. And we can be proud of being the living generation of following our Gurus' teachings. This is what we have talked about all our life and this is what made me choose a military career, together with you and the support of your dad.
Jassi:	All this is true. But discourses with your sister Guddi from time to time during and after completing our master's left me

introspecting about developing my own values as well. They have started evolving.

Guddu: My sister claims she is revolutionary minded. She is too loud for her own good. She has read Gaskell's *Mary Barton*, Karl Marx and some of the pseudo-revolutionary poetry of Heinrich Heine and compares the conditions of ordinary people there to the conditions here and she is moved. But dad likes her free-moving thought and her devotion to improving human conditions. And that is why she talks to you on these issues.

Jassi: I have concluded that the real meaningful values of life are at variance with the values of the military. And the fundamental values of our gurus also lie in a life other than the military. The military-type life is only to defend the honour and faith of our community. But this military training and military ethos we have had had nothing to do with these values.

Guddu: Your revelation is both true and shocking, but I guess, on reflection, it is very true.

Jassi: I'm sorry.

Guddu: You have to remain in the army.

Jassi: *Why?*

Guddu: Because I joined it because of all the encouragement I received from you and your dad.

Jassi: I know. I'm sorry.

Guddu: We have the strength of mind and body that people envy us. While we must uphold the altruistic and humanitarian values of our gurus, you cannot at this stage just give up your joining of the army. Jassi, I am telling you, for the sake of our families, an about turn from you at this time is just not acceptable. Give up any thoughts of not remaining in the army. Remain for now in the army and you may be able to review your life objectives in a few years. We have to display stability in our thinking and cannot be seen to be impulsive in our approach to life.

Jassi:	It is because of the commitment that I have informally with you that I am still in the army. But, yes, as Guddi says, do I have to serve the imperial government whose only value is to amass wealth at the expense of our ordinary people, using cruel means of control whenever they decide to? I have been questioning this very vigorously.
Guddu:	But no, Jassi, you are not leaving the army for now in any case. We will continue this discussion later.
Jassi:	I'm serious Guddu.
Guddu:	We will discuss it later.
Jassi:	There is nothing to discuss –
Guddu:	Jassi, listen to me. Listen to me. My sister doesn't know what she's talking about. She's a woman for a start and full of new-fangled anger against the Empire, no different from the liberal European thought that we read in our master's course. Her tongue can be sharp, and she is young and utopian. You do not want to be influenced by a utopian for your future. You are a soldier Jassi. Like me. We are both soldiers. Best friends do not betray like this Jassi. It is not what they do.

Guddu and Jassi walk in to the tented ground of the party

Jassi:	Ready?
Guddu:	To start our lives at last? Of course. Open those doors, my dearest friend Jassi.
Pammi:	(V/O) We were ready? I don't know now. I knew I was ready for something. But I had no idea what. Who does at that age?

Jassi opens the doors into the party. A huge cheer goes up.
Sudden applause breaks out. Jassi and Guddu enter in their most colourful kurtas and shining turbans with some military regalia of their regiment.

Rani:	Guddi – Guddi –Oh my god …!…!…!… Guddu is looking awfully handsome. Did you guide him for tonight?

Guddi: Well ... my brother ... is ... always handsome (*she says jokingly and laughs*) and so is Jassi.

Beat.

Gurnam: A bit of quiet please. Here we are. May I introduce you to these extremely talented two youngsters, who, through thick and thin, have been together all these years and are now celebrating the end of their education career. And they have chosen military careers, passed their training as officers and will shortly lead their men, going into practical army life. Fully marriageable age. Ladies and Gentlemen ... GUDDU AND JASSI ...

(applause breaks out and as it dies)

Jaspreet: Or ... may I say in reverse ... JASSI AND GUDDU ... (*everyone's laughter breaks out*), not really, both are equal to me and inseparable. It has been my life's great pleasure to see these two together in the way they have been all their lives. Now let us have some Bhangra and get the joyfulness into full swing.

Gurnam: Come, Jaspreet, let us watch these young people enjoy their version of modern enjoyment.

(Music and dancing continues. At times, Jassi and Guddi and, separately, Rani and Guddu, get into some conversation)

Guddi: Jassi virji, how do you feel about this merriment?

Jassi: We could not have imagined anything better.

Guddi: What a pity that you have to join the army, the repressive arm of the foreign rulers.

Jassi: *Don't say these words.*

Guddi: Why not? It's true, isn't it?

Jassi: No.

Guddi: You're in denial.

Jassi: Guddi please –

Guddi: I know you Jassi –

Jassi: You don't know me enough –

Guddi: You heard me when I spoke to you, and now you have doubts –

Jassi: Stop –

Guddi: Don't you –

Jassi: (staring though regretfully) Stop Guddi please –
Silence. Party stops briefly.
Jassi: Please. (*to the crowd*) TO OUR NEW CAREERS IN
                    THE ARMY!
(All cheer)
Guddi: Liar.
Jassi: You're right. Everything you say, you're right.
Guddi: So take off the uniform.
Jassi: I can't.
Guddi: Before it's too late.
Jassi: Over these last three months, having seen the actual army
                    life, I have come to feel that an army career is deeply offensive
                    and alien to me. I know you have spoken to me on several
                    occasions of the need to defend our people against oppres-
                    sion by English rulers. Your ideas never really clicked with
                    me even though I have been appreciating what you have been
                    saying. Though, about now, seeing how the army ethos con-
                    flicts with my own inner urges, I can see some validity of
                    your thinking. Yet that alone is not a factor in my disavowing
                    of army life. The whole ethos of fighting, fighting, etc. is a bit
                    revolting to my conscience. I would fight to defend my family
                    and my loved ones, but the current army ethos, whether it is
                    the Indian army or the British army in India, is fighting for the
                    sake of fighting. This is what is intolerable.
Guddi: Let us talk more later. For now carry on the merriment.
*They carry on their Bhangra and Gidda to the dance tunes. At the other end of the
Hall, Guddu is engaged in some conversation with Rani.*
Guddu: You have done a magnificent job of this event. So beautifully
                    decorated and such a great team of musicians, not to say much
                    of the amazing dishes available.
Rani: For fine people, we have to do the finest thing. And you are
                    finest of all. So we had no choice but to show our great love
                    for you. And with Guddi arranging it for you, how could it not
                    be the best.

Guddu: Most unforgettable scene. See how everyone is so happy and enjoying every moment.

Rani: Well that is what we planned for. After all our brothers have a new stage of life. Are you also set for the army awaiting your commission?

Guddu: Most certainly. A great adventurous career to begin with. Guddi is not happy about my choice. Dad is fine, but less than fully happy. Mum wants to see her son safe and developing a family. But Jassi and I are committed.

Rani: Whatever others seek of you, I wish you well and want to see you thriving … and who knows what is in store for us.

Guddu: A veiled desire from you has also seeped in? I suppose your dad has mentioned it to you. Our dads have been talking about it. It seems that you got the smell of it and have started imagining your future … with me. But for the moment, let me go in for more of bash of today, to enjoy the best of what you have created for us.

After some more music and bhangra, Jaspreet seeks to say a few words

Jaspreet: Folks, Gurnam and I knew when we floated the idea of a party that we may be doing something that has not been done before. But both of us are very proud of the work done by our daughters for their brothers. It surpasses the best of ours, and I am sure, all of your expectations.

                These two boys, talented, and may I say very handsome lads, strong of physique and mental strength, have shown their talents, having passed the master's degree from the best college in the land. And they have completed their officers' training in the army. I want those talents now to be deployed for the good of all of us. I had always earmarked them for an army career. But recently, Jassi has shown serious doubts that this is the right career for **him**.

Jassi: *What's he saying?*

Guddi: The truth —

Jaspreet: He has deep objections to the ethos of the army.

Jassi: *(blushing)* Father please –

Guddi: Tell him now how you feel –

Jassi: Guddi … please …

Jaspreet: But I insist that for the honour of our family, he has no choice but to join the army.

Guddi: *(to Gurnam)* That's not fair.

Sighs from all around.

Gurnam: Let him speak, Guddi –

Jassi: Guddi please –

Guddi: It's the truth – please let me express the truth openly

Gurnam: Let your magnificent work remain so. Do not spoil what you have achieved so wonderfully,

Guddi: Fine.

Guddi starts to walk away.

She leaves the room.

Silence.

Jaspreet: *(awkwardly)* So, *ladies and gentlemen* join me in sending the best of wishes to these two stalwarts for a happy life to come.

There is an awkward cheer.

SCENE 3

Gurnam:	The party is going well.
Jaspreet:	This is an understatement. For once, let your modesty and realism mix up.
Gurnam:	The party has been great.
Jaspreet:	I have enjoyed it thoroughly.
Gurnam:	Is Jassi really having second thoughts?
Jaspreet:	It seems so. With all due respect to you, we have a family tradition to maintain and I cannot throw it overboard. Personal wishes take second place to a family tradition. So Jassi has to follow it.
Gurnam:	Of the two boys I would have thought it would be Guddu who would have doubts. But if Jassi has doubts, it is praiseworthy, given your own family discipline that he has had to live through.
Jaspreet:	Well, there is no choice. This has to be the case.
Gurnam:	She is forever projecting utopian and Marxist thoughts and it is surely disdainful towards the Empire and I am sorry for this — at least in respect of the cases that I handle day in and day out.
Jaspreet:	Our sons will both be joining the Army my friend. Let us two not fight over such nonsense.
Gurnam:	But if Jaspreet does have his doubts —
Jaspreet:	Having doubts is not enough to loosen discipline. Enough said. No more on the matter. Case is closed.
Pammi:	*(V/O) But Jassi did have doubts. And they ran deep. So deep that even I, his dearest friend could not see. Or even if I could, I refused to believe them. How could I have been so stupid?*

SCENE 4

A few days later, at home with Jassi, Rani and Jassi's mum, around the morning tea in the plush garden.

Jaspreet: Breaking stories in the newspapers. So war has finally broken out in Europe.

Jassi: What does that mean, Father?

Jaspreet: It means that we too are at war, Son.

Jassi: Why so?

Jaspreet: We are part of the British Empire and therefore as subjects of the King, we will obey wartime orders.

Jassi: Even though we are thousands of miles from them?

Jaspreet: Look, Son, we have never had as much peace as we have had in the last 60 years. We owe it to the British rule. So we, as subjects of the Crown owe them and ourselves the protection of the realm.

Rani: So what does the news mean for these two boys?

Jaspreet: It means that my discussions with Gurnam about your match with Guddu will be put at rest.

(Rani blushes)

Jassi: Father —

Jaspreet: You are part of the Army now, Son, and so duty calls.

Silence.

Jaspreet: It is time now.

Jassi: Yes.

Jaspreet: It is time. Don't tease her more than she can take. This news certainly places her own future life in some kind of confusion. But we will take care. She is at an age where we need not wait too long.

(Guddu comes in)

Jassi: I thought that I had some time to make a final decision about whether to continue in the army or not. It seems from dad's speech that I may have no choice. But this war news has left me with no choice. A bit shattered, really.

Guddu: So the decision has been made and we will go arm in arm into the army to do our duty on the field. Remember Banda Bahadur acting for our Guru fighting to defend our faith and honour at Sirhind? Singlehandedly he repulsed the Mughals because he was driven by defending the faith. We have to go into battle with the same spirit. Whatever their faults, the English have also been good to us in many ways. Let us focus on that.

Jassi: This is a new situation and my doubts take a second place. We are arm in arm and will remain together. But only for this emerging situation. If I find something obnoxious, I will want to take steps to walk away should the situation permit.

Jaspreet: In the current situation, young able-bodied people, as subjects of the crown, have little choice. They will have to make themselves available for army duties. And you have to do that with pride. And, you are lucky. You have had three months' officers' training and that may put you in line for getting rapid promotion to lead your men into battle. I better go to my staff HQ right away.

SCENE 5

Jaspreet leaves the scene. Jassi and Guddu decide to go out towards the city

Jassi: I have agreed to join the army. I may still decline. But it is more than that. It is the values that lie behind what she says even though she does not articulate this aspect well.

Guddu: You can live for those values even after you have had a stint in the army. For now you have given your word. There is no going back. And certainly not at this hour of war.

Jassi: I think you too should think whether to join the army or not. Can we not help our people without joining the army?

Guddu: Yes. We will. For now at this hour we have no choice. Our friendship should have value and let us show our commitment to it at this hour as well. After all, your dad has let you know the value of the family tradition. We just cannot ignore it, and the least of yourself, cannot ignore it. For now, let us assume that you have to join the army and let us go to the bazaar and have fun.

Jassi: Yes. Let us relax a bit in the heart of the Heera Mandi district. Between you and dad, the pressure that I am seeing to join seems irresistible in any case.

Pammi: *(V/O) How could I have been so stupid?*

SCENE 6

- -

Jassi finds time to discuss the broader issues with Guddi

Guddi: I am sorry I embarrassed you in front of all those people. I say stuff. Too much. I'm sorry.

Jassi: But you were right. I feel that you are actually the only person who is right.

Guddi: It is difficult for me to solve your predicament. Awful situation to be in. But I am dead against helping the imperial rulers allowing them to rule so brutally over us. I will not encourage anyone to join the army. But with mobilization in the offing, you may have no choice. You will have to go.

Jassi: Well, yes. You will maintain your freedom. And even if you write to me about your deeds against the government, the letters will be censored. But our gurus' teaching will always remain a great source of strength to me to act correctly, whether in performing my duty or maintaining my thoughts.

Guddi: So go. Go with a clear mind and clear conscience. You know that my thoughts will always be with you. But keep in mind that as soon as you get your discharge, the human values with which you are now imbibed will be your driving force in life.

SCENE 7

Both the families get together the next day — Jaspreet, Gurnam, Jassi, Guddu, Guddi and Rani

Jaspreet: Sons, it is time for you to make your final preparations to go to Europe. Remember that you have been called for because every healthy young subject of the Crown has an obligation to defend the Crown. But you in particular are from the elite fighting force. You are fearless soldiers dedicated to delivering the fighting qualities. Your bravery will be a badge of honour for all of us.

Gurnam: I cannot add more though with some reservations. But remember that you are going as descendants of our great gurus and their teachings. You must uphold them.

Guddu: I am excited. But I have only one regret. We have not been able to taste the love, prestige and respect that our friends and people bestow on army officers.

Jassi: What can I say. I have no choice but to join Guddu in pursuance of our responsibilities generated by this new situation. We will show our mettle.

Rani: I never imagined that we would have to part company for indefinite and probably long periods at this critical junctures of our lives. We have hopes in you both and all other men and officers who have placed their lives in the service of the King.

Guddi: The King has placed an unjust demand on all of us. I do not have any sympathy with his demands. May God protect you all. The King will not.

Guddu: I can feel your sentiments, Guddi. But we have no choice having gone through officers' training. We were mobilized automatically. But have heart. It is for all of you that we are going.

SCENE 8

Guddu and Jassi depart for their barracks. Guddi and Rani wave, with tears filling their eyes

Guddu: Jassi, we have a few days before leaving. We can slip out at night to enjoy the Lahore nightlife.

Jassi: Let us experience the other side of life in India before we depart. Don't tell mum and dad about this ... shhhhhhhhhhhhhhhhh ...

Guddu: Good. Let us taste it. Full of the most titillating ghazals. And great romantic environment.

Jassi: Got to be careful. I would like to avoid my dad's friends spotting us.

Guddu: If they come, that means they too have such tastes. So what's the problem?

Jassi: You have answers to every potentially embarrassing situation.

Guddu: Fear not anything my dear Jassi. Our gurus have taught us to face the truth fearlessly.

Jassi: Will do my best given the situation.

Guddu: We have this pleasure of the nightlife here only because we are officer corps. Nice feeling that we can set some agenda for ourselves, responsibly in respect to our duty obligations of course.

Jassi: The music over here is awfully beautiful. And these nightlife birds sing so naturally.

Guddu: This is what I wanted to experience.

Jassi: We could not have enjoyed this outing had we not been officers in the army, at least not at this point in our lives.

Guddu: It has been an excellent and a most memorable night. Let us get back to where we have to be, at our camp near the port. We got to be ready and smart before daybreak.

Pammi: *(V/O) It was the last night we spent so young, so fresh, so happy. After that night, we were soldiers, and we were going to war.*

ACT 3

SCENE 1

-- -- -- -- -- -- -- -- -- -- -- -- -- -- --

The troopship

Guddu: Ow.

Jassi: Never has my head felt like this. And why is the sea making this boat move so much?

Guddu: I don't think it is the sea, my friend, that's moving.

Jassi: Why did you keep me out so late last night?

Guddu: Come on, Jassi ... it is worth every pain in my whole body right now. What a night.

Jassi: Have you seen your men yet?

Guddu: Of course.

Jassi: And how are they?

Guddu: All set. My men are in trim shape. There is some fear in some of them. But we will lead them into battle fearlessly.

Jassi: My men too are in trim shape. Many of them are hoping that they will be doing a great service to their families by generating regular income for them. Some are seeking an adventure.

Guddu: Look, I feel strong to go and not concerned about anything. But it did come to my mind that some of them will not come back. This is the last they are seeing of their beloved families. And that may be myself too. Rani was left in tears as we left.

Jassi: I too have similar thoughts. But all of you gagged me. I just wonder if the blood spill and life sacrifices will bring happiness to their families. What do they expect to gain in all this – a few pennies worth of living?

Guddu: Who can ignore what you say? But this is war. As subjects of our imperial rulers, we have to participate and that too without demurring.

Jassi: This is what Guddi has been telling me all the time. Whose war? It will remotely protect our families if we prevent the

Germans taking over India. But beyond this, how does His
Excellency the King give our families and people something
in exchange for, in some cases, ruining families?

Guddu: So it is incumbent upon us to creatively keep our men in positive spirits and forward looking. We will make representations whenever possible.

Jassi: But in wartime, we may rarely have a good chance to make
representations. Nonetheless, we need to move forward and
hope for a quick end to the war.

Guddu: Let us enthuse our men and help them to remain upbeat, as
our guru has always taught us.

Jassi: I will sneak out the night before embarking to say bye to our
families once again. Not an easy task that we have undertaken.
Leaving our families all of a sudden after having spent all our
lives full of love and care.

SCENE 2

- -

On board the troopship as the troopship leaves the harbour.

Guddu: A long voyage but we may break up in Alexandria for a couple of days.

Jassi: I have heard many stories about Alexandria from some of my officers.

Guddu: What type?

Jassi: They used to talk in very luscious tones. Made we wonder the type of people there.

Guddu: I would love to see the life of freedom there and the free-wheeling opposite sex adventures.

Jassi: Even ten days to Alexandria on sea can be a tough test.

Guddu: But we need to make it an exciting journey.

Pammi: *(V/O) And so we sang. We sang to make our journey exciting.*

Jassi: Daily training is a must. We must shape our men's expectations of the job ahead.

Guddu: And I will add entertainment while on board. They get excited by the thought of folk songs recalling the most beautiful women and only in imagination, they longed for and could not get them.

They sing

BANNEY LAGAN DI NA DER
PAHUNCHEY SIKANDER -E-BANDAR
BAN GAYA SABH AAS PASS
IK PHULLAN DA SAMUNDAR
KHABEY, GABBEY, SAJJEY JAVAN CHAROO HIS PASSEY
DHUMAKDA DHUMAKDA, GORIYAN GALLAN DA PORBANDER

Jassi: Once more! Once more, what a joy. Alexandria has cata-
              pulted these simple young men into purveyors of romance.
Guddu: They could never have dreamed of this freedom back home.
              The feel of another female – boy – has lifted these men to this
              previously unimaginable joy.
Jassi: Now back to serious stuff. We need to prepare to disembark
              in style for the parade. Let us get our men ready.

SCENE 3

From the ship to the camp just outside Marseilles

Guddu: Unbelievable. The three-hour march past from the ship to the camp. Have never seen such a rapturous welcome, particularly from women. And so many of them, by tens of thousands. Back home not one would dare to come out. They would be proud of us though, but inside the four walls.

Jassi: I could not believe so many women kissing us and our men. I loved those kisses. And I could not stop wishing for more and more of them. How delicious they were. And they were vying with one another to kiss us. And women were trying to grab us. OH! What an experience. How will I describe this experience in my letters home.

Guddu: So coming over here with me now has had additional benefits to you, more than in Alexandria. And do you know that the C-in-C of the French armed forces took the salute. That is perhaps why Gen Kitchener led the parade for us.

Jassi: And we have been treated with great respect. Great feeling.

Guddu: Let us get our men together and get their experiences. It is worth capturing these emotions to be recorded in the annals of wartime history.

In the company of both the battalions (Jassi / Guddu battalions)

Guddu: My *jawans*, you are now in the heart of Europe. Did you enjoy the welcome?

All the men: Yeah. Excellent. Could not imagine such a welcome ever existed.

Jassi: Now get ready. The welcome was a hearty thank you to you all. And that must make you all feel special. And we now have to act special too, worthy of the welcome. We are here for a purpose and I want you all to get home as soon as possible after we have accomplished our mission.

All the men: Yeah! Yeah! Yeah!

Guddu: Get to know your new surroundings. We will provide you with plans tomorrow. In the meantime enjoy your evening with your bumper party. The food chefs have been working hard to give you a truly big party tonight.

SCENE 4

Troops move on to Orleans and beyond for staging. The Commanding Officer receives them all.

Guddu: Comrades, you got familiar with France a little bit in Marseilles. Here in Orleans, you will get used to the colder weather and the harsh surroundings on the battlefield. Nothing is beyond your reach.

Jassi: Hey, it is cold here. We do need some proper clothing. The train coaches were well heated. How do we get heating in the camps?

Guddu: I have sent my aide-de-camp to the quartermaster already.

Jassi: And remember, only the strong can survive. You are all here because you are strong. Remember the strong – Banda Bahadur at Sirhind with only a handful, he survived the onslaught of 10,000 Mughals; and remember about 30 years ago in Afghanistan, 10,000 Afghans were held at bay by only 10 Sikh soldiers. You are all here because of the strength that history has taught you.

Guddu: And I want all of you to go through this excruciating cold weather, barefoot, without clothing and at times with clothing. You are going to go through all this in the coming days. Get used to all of this.

Pammi: *(V/O) But after the song, the men would still be asking why they were there.*

A Private Sergeant 1: What are we preparing to fight and why?

Another Private Sergeant 2: Shut up you silly idiot. We have been told all the stories about this during our voyage and you are still asking?

Sergeant 1:	Look, I miss my family. I do not find a reason good enough for why I should not miss them.
Jassi:	You milk sucking son of your mum. Grow up. You have a duty to perform here. We are fighting a war with Germany. Only by surviving and winning this war will our families be safe back home. So get ready to fight to protect your family.

SCENE 5

After two weeks of acclimatization and training the urgent need to resist the advance of German troops are now moved to the front and thrown into battle.

Pammi: *(V/O) And then very quickly we landed. Suddenly home felt a long way away. Our fathers, our mothers, the parties and the hope. Suddenly we were here in France. And we were scared. And we were cold. It was so very cold.*

Jassi: Comrades! Get ready. We are moving to the front in less than an hour. All of you should gather on the parade area here.

Sergeant 1:   Give us proper clothing sir. It is too cold.

Jassi: Can you find Himmat, my adjutant? He had gone to the quartermaster to get all the supplies. Let me see how Captain Guddu is handling the situation and I will be back.

Jassi goes to see Guddu and gets into an argument

Jassi: Tensions are rising, Guddu. Men are getting restive. They are very uncomfortable in this weather. They are swearing left, right and center. I have not seen them this agitated any time so far.

Guddu: I have been to the quartermaster. And made it clear to that motherfucker to get things right. I am working at it and you too need to put your weight in getting the supplies.

Jassi: The facilities over here have really generated anger. All are swearing in the name of mothers, sisters and any woman all over, with every sentence. It is as if that the British have sent us all for punishment over here. Guddi had a point, is it not? So obvious.

Guddu: Oh Jassi – stop that. Let us find solutions.

Jassi: Only if they let us find them. Do you see how well dressed the French soldiers and British officers are?

Guddu: We have to be moving soon. Let me get the best out of the QM depot.

Jassi: The quartermaster is at it. Your rations and clothing are on the way.

Sergeant 2: And what about the weapons. We have not had the chance to try them out in this weather. Will they work?

Jassi: We are taking care. A good and continuous supply of weapons and other equipment is being prepared. You will be a fine fighting machine.

Sergeant 1: (*To other members of the battalion*) I had heard that the fighting preparation in Europe was top notch. But we seem to be less equipped than we were generally in Indian Afghan wars. There also it was very cold.

Jassi: Go run to the quartermaster camp and give them the list of things we want.

Make the list and show it to me before you go. I will see you in a moment.

Sergeant 2: Let us not now focus on these things. The officers are not throwing us into battle only to be killed. We are expected to defeat the enemy, even if we have to kill them. They know that we should be equipped with the relevant equipment. So let us hope for the best.

Sergeant 1: All is well that ends well. I want to be with my family soonest.

Jassi goes back to see Guddu immediately, who is not far from him

Guddu: Jassi, you are here and you seem a bit agitated. Why?

Jassi: My men are still asking for equipment and warm clothing and I do not have an answer to that. Are we so poorly prepared to go into battle?

Guddu: Jassi, let us do the best. Things are not at their best and an emergency fighting situation has arisen. We cannot run away from the situation. One of the problems that we must handle successfully is these emergency situations.

Jassi: This is where I am failing. Perhaps my doubts of coming here are taking the better of me.

Guddu: We are in this situation, do we have any options?

Jassi: I want to do the best for my men. I have as much a responsibility for my men as for my duty. All this is happening because the seniors have no respect for us Indians. Many of those who are training us have seen Indians for the first time. But preparing with basic equipment is part of the very basics of military supplies. They should know that at least. Or is it they know about it and they just do not care?

Guddu: Let us make proper representations and not let emotions get the better of us.

SCENE 6

The CO comes in, everyone stands to attention.

CO: I have just received a telegraphic message. Your battalion has been assigned to the front at La Neuve Chapelle. We are about six hours by train from here. So get ready for it tomorrow.

Jassi: And before we depart for the next station, we will have a hearty dinner and dance. Get ready for it in one hour.

Sergeant 1: What about our twin battalion? We have soldiers from our village there. Get them also for the dinner.

Jassi: Done.

Sergeant 1: I hope that we will march together with them.

Here — music in background — Guddu has been dancing, but Jassi has not. He is not able to get into the mood. Guddu finds him and sits with him. A moment of clarity. Jassi asks Guddu to look out for him, and Guddu says that he will always look out for him. Guddu makes that promise. Reluctantly.

After dinner, they all go to their tents to prepare for departure early the next morning. Guddu's and Jassi's battalions are together. After a full day's train journey, they get lodged in a camp not far from the front in the Ypres Salient. At nightfall the next day, they take up positions on the front.

Battle of La Bassees

Guddu: *Jawanon*, we are now at the front. Keep low and start digging the trenches. No time to waste.

Jassi: Everyone, lie down. Heavy bombardment likely to continue. Just been told that there is a large German force in front. Down! Down!

Sergeant 1: Never heard such heavy bombardment. Is the heaven falling on us?

Sergeant 2: Ouch! A heavy shell. God help. I am fine.

Jassi: I need to go right in front of the battalion. Guddu, take care.

Guddu:	I am also going to take the lead in front. Whoosh! Whoosh! Whoosh! Bullets flying right across us. IT IS REALLY DEADLY ...
Jassi:	I may see you at the back during some rest period. Bye. Take care.
Guddu:	Whoom! A large explosion just in front. Any one injured? We will be a fort like wall to these *bhainchod* Germans.
Sergeant:	No reports of any casualties for the moment. Keeping up.
Guddu:	Remember, only the brave survive. We are all brave. Get into trenches, even if shallow for the moment. These *mader chod* have to be shown who we are. We must get this shelling stopped – only by killing the enemy or direct hit to their equipment.
Sergeant:	We are staying put, but it is very cold. Fingers are frozen. Cannot move.
Guddu:	Someone is bringing some warmth very shortly. Stay put.

Pammi:	*(V/O) For three days the Indian Army fought hard. So much so, that the Germans started to think twice. We were good. We were hard. And brave. We were so brave as a nation of soldiers. A group of soldiers so far from home.*

After three days almost exclusively at the front, with food and supplies delivered there, the battalions withdrew, the fighting had died down

The Corp Commander: Your brave men have endured a very tough fight. But this time, I suppose they had no reason to be wary. Food and other supplies were supplied in plenty.

Lahore Division Commander: I guess you are right. I did not hear much of a complaint about food and other supplies.

The Corp Commander: (*to Lahore division commander*) There seems to be a lull in fighting. Your division has vitally helped us to halt the progress of the Germans. Well done. I hope the lull is not much of a tactical move but a realization by the Germans that they will not make much headway here.

Lahore Division Commander: We have brave fighting men. Did you get reports of how soldiers like Khudad Khan single-handedly fought off the Germans? We were desperately outnumbered and under massive constant German attacks

The Corp Commander: And he has been recommended for the very highest medal of bravery, the Victoria Cross. And they helped us maintain the critical rail and road junctions just at Ypres.

Lahore Division Commander: And my men fought, though better supplied, but nevertheless without adequate protection from the cold. We need to rectify this immediately. The casualty rate has been enormous.

The Corp Commander: Get them proper R&R

Lahore Division Commander: We have recruited some wonderful hosts who have voluntarily offered their homes for the officer corp. We will use these offers for these brave fighters.

The Guddu and Jassi battalions were back in their camps as the fighting died down in late November 1914, tired and exhausted. Guddu and Jassi were housed in the comfortable homes of English-speaking French ladies who had willingly and voluntarily offered their homes for front line officers. They are at a dinner party, in February 1915, with Emily, the hostess who had hosted Jassi. She was mesmerized with him and had prepared a sumptuous party for Guddu and Jassi and invited a few of her neighbours as well. Guddu's hostess, Alice, was also present.

Jassi: I knocked at Emily's house to have a nice rest and sleep. She has been very great moral and spiritual support of us Indian soldiers and goes out of her way to deliver comfort to me whenever I see her.

Guddu: These ladies are wonderful. Aren't they.

Jassi: Exactly. She laid out a beautiful sumptuous breakfast (mind you no *paranthas!!!*) and told me that they have a huge get together and party for the officers of our corps this evening.

Guddu: Oh yes. This is what Alicia was saying too. Let us see what experience we will have this evening.

Jassi: But Emily has opened up with me. She treats me like God. She says that she prays for me all the time that I remain safe.

	And, above all, I enjoy her intimacy with me, lovely hugs and kisses AND something more too …
Guddu:	You *bastard*. You are upto something. Keep going. It will keep your morale going up.
Emily:	These soldiers have seen fierce fighting. I wonder how they go through all this.
Alice:	Indeed.
Guddu:	From what we hear, we are preparing for even more fierce fighting once the snows melt a bit.
Jassi:	Yes, we hear that the German soldiers are massing up in huge numbers. We do not know in what direction they will attack.
Guddu:	And of course we are also preparing our plan to confront them. Our commanders are working hard to make sense of the German tactics.
Emily:	Whatever, I feel so thankful to you soldiers who have come very far from your homes and are away from your families to protect us from the Germans. I do not know how to thank you.
Jassi:	It is your love and affection that you have showered on us that sustains our fighting spirit. All love is a great force. But your love and affection for me is very genuine, though not having been used to this kind of intimacy from non-family members back home, it took me by pleasant surprise. I appreciated every moment of your hearty and affectionate welcome from our first contact. And this is a great incentive for displaying our courage on the battlefield.
Guddu:	And I second that fully. What we are doing is what our gurus have taught us. Give your best to protect the weaker elements of society. And you women, the remnants of broken families because your men have perished in the battle, are surely the weaker elements. So we are duty bound to do the best for you.
Alice:	I feel the same way as Emily. But now, Emily it seems, is fully romantically involved with Jassi. She never stops talking about him. And in such lovely expressions of love. How lucky both of you.

Guddu: Alice, I am sure that it is only your age that has prevented you into falling romantically for me. But you are still young enough for us to enjoy some romance and physical intimacy. But every gesture and expression of your care towards me is full of so much affection and care. It melts me. Your affection and love is more than romance for me.

Jassi: You have made us feel so cosy, Emily and Alice. We can only thank our stars. But after tonight, we have to go to the front to take up new positions. But our thoughts will always be with you all. We are part of you now and feel so.

Guddu: We have had two months' of extreme comfort. It never felt like war.

Jassi: I have felt like this is my new home.

Guddu: Yes. But now back to the front.

Pammi: *(V/O) For a brief period we were housed in a beautiful French house with the most wonderful hosts. But this didn't last. No sooner had we arrived than we were sent back to the front. We were needed. The Germans were advancing and we were needed. But both Jassi and I for a brief moment were looked after so well. It was peaceful. And comfortable. We were finally able to rest. And we were lucky. Our hosts were probably two of the most prettiest ladies in all of France. We were in love!*

SCENE 7

- - - - - - - - - - - - - - - - - - - -

The restructured Indian corps is now deployed for the forthcoming Battles of <u>Neuve Chapelle</u>, <u>Aubers Ridge</u>, <u>Festubert</u> and <u>Loos</u> in 1915. GOC: Maj-Gen <u>H. D'U. Keary</u>. Jassi and Guddu are assigned to the Jullunder Brigade and both are moved to the 47th Sikh. Violent and brutal fighting breaks out.

Guddu: After an excellent rest and recuperation, we are back in the trenches. But in the midst of reorganized units. General Sir, we are so happy to have the honour of you being with our Jullunder Brigade.

Commandng Officer: That is right. Jullunder Brigade has developed a huge reputation of bravery and I want to ensure that the higher ups recognize your brave feats.

Guddu: We are far better clothed and equipped than during the last battle. And it is less cold now.

Commandng Officer: It is the same for the other side. And they too have prepared for the forthcoming battle.

Guddu: If we faced them bravely the last time, it will be even more fierce this time to deliver our orders on the battlefield.

Commanding Officer: Ultimately it was a battle of wills at Ypres and your division performed extremely well. With experience behind us now, we expect your men under your good leadership to perform even better.

Jassi: We have a lot of bravery and will power. Despite my regiment having been very severely bloodied in *La Bassée, Messines and Armentières,* fighting on the front to perform our duties becomes ever more important for us in honour of our fallen comrades. But I still have the same nagging question: what are we fighting for? And why?

Guddu:	Jassi, if this question is still nagging you, let us discuss after this engagement. You have seen both the good aspects of being here (Emily is now for sure your aimant, and you are somewhat over the moon for that) and the bad side. So let us talk through in a few days.
Jassi:	Very well, I am off to my men to see that they are properly amused and incentivized for the engagement that we all expect.

As soon as Jassi and Guddu arrive to be with their men, severe fighting erupts.

Jassi:	My *faujis* (soldiers), lie low. Do not move.
Fauji:	*Whoosh, whoosh, whoosh.* Is the heaven falling down? This noise and thunder, never ending, ever increasing in ferocity? Sending fright through even the hardiest soldier.
Jassi:	Stay where you are. Do not fire until commanded.
Sergeant:	Yes. Yes. But they seem to be coming nearer and nearer.
Jassi:	They do not know that we are here. We will be firing soon and they come nearer and our fire power can reach them.
Sergeant:	*Whoosh!!!* Are you alright sir? This is very heavy shelling indeed (*Boom Boom*). Why have our bosses allowed these motherfuckers to bring all these weapons near us. *Ooooooooooooooooooch* — my orderly has had a direct hit.
Jassi:	Yes I am alright. I need to go a bit further up. If you are covered, can you scramble a bit forward.?
Sergeant 1:	*Bahadron (the brave ones),* inch up forward. *Boom! Boom! Boom!* Do not worry. Only the brave win and we must win. These sons of bitches *kudi chod* will not be able to pass us.
Sergeant 2:	I am holding but Captain Jassi has had a direct hit. Out of the blue. He was trying to improve our defence in the front.
Sergeant 1:	Evacuate him immediately. I have sent a message to the controlling officer to take our boss back, I will replace Jassi for the moment.
Pammi:	*(V/O) In three days of fighting at the front, with rest only in the trenches, the battalion took a severe beating. Worst of all, Jassi was*

severely injured and had to be evacuated for emergency treatment and sent to Brighton for recovery. He had taken a near direct hit and his backbone was severely damaged. A few days after the evacuation, my battalion, severely mauled but still intact, was brought in for rest. I became aware of Jassi's situation and could not rest still for the next few days when I learnt that he had been admitted to the Brighton hospital for treatment

Guddu: Back to some senses. Continuous bombardment takes the hell out of a person.

Commanding Officer: This is what rotation of troops is meant for. It can be very stressful. You know that Jassi has been evacuated to Brighton for treatment. He took a serious hit.

Guddu: Oh my god. This is the last thing I wanted to happen. Not to him. I had rather it happened to me. I must try and go to see him.

Commanding Officer: Wait a few days. I will see if some arrangements can be made.

Guddu: But I do need to know about the state of his injury. I have a special duty of responsibility to him.

Commanding Officer: I am aware of your link with him. We will do something to assuage your concern. We are proud of you and your unit. You have held the ground despite overwhelmingly crushing odds.

Guddu: I can bear all the pain at the front. But Jassi's pain is unbearable for me.

Commanding Officer: A professional risk, I am afraid. But as an officer, you must remain brave. You cannot let this pain affect your determination.

Guddu: No. That will not happen. But please do not trivialize my pain. The pain reflects not only our friendship since childhood, but also the loss of chance to help put into practice the humanitarianism of evolving values that were going through Jassi's mind. And though they were overwhelming him, he came to this theatre only due to me against his own instincts. And these thoughts are very painful to me.

Commanding Officer: Well I can only sympathize with you and move ahead. Do not think that I am only cold blooded in my thinking, but more immediate issues need to be addressed. General Wilcox has been informed of your exemplary bravery and I am sure some medals are on the way for Jassi and also yourself.

Guddu: Alright, moving ahead, I have promised my men good rest and hearty meals. I suppose we have a week of rest before we move back again.

Commanding Officer: I am at your disposal to provide any comfort I can for your men. Do not hesitate. And remember,

After some rest and recuperation, Guddu and his men are thrown into battle.

Fauji: Sir, I am fed up of these very difficult fighting conditions. No proper guns. No proper clothing to this weather which changes without warning.

Guddu: If you keep on talking like this, you will not only be a dishonour to us all, but I may have to send you to court martial.

Another Fauji: Can we not get proper weapons to beat the enemy? They come up with fast firing weapons with massive destructive effect. We are nowhere near them.

Guddu: Come *bahadur*, get on. We do what we can. Those weapons are nothing against our spirits.

Fauji: Oh! Bastard, a bullet hit my turban. *Wahe guru ka khalsa.*

Guddu: Take care. Do not expose yourself. Stay still. Our job is to defend our post till the last breath.

Fauji: Now that we are here, we will only move forward or remain here. The cold weather does not help. But we are here. Count on us.

Pammi: *(V/O) Within minutes, Boom! Heavy mortar falls. Nearby. No one injured. The battle continues. After a few days, just a few minutes before my battalion was supposed to pull back for rest, heavy firing began with mortars. One of the mortars fell right near me. I was*

*sent flying a few meters behind the lines. I was severely injured, and
received prompt care by the medics.*

Fauji:　　Captain Sahib, oh my god!!. What a shock. You have been hit!
Ranjit, please pick Captain Sahib immediately and take him
to medics.

Pammi:　　*(V/O) I was transferred to the hospital in Brighton. The South Coast
of England. Seagulls. And beaches with stones. And wind. Always
there was a wind.*

ACT 4

SCENE 1

- - - - - - - - - - - - - - - - - - -

Lucy:	Hello, my name is Lucy.
Guddu:	I have a friend.
Lucy:	Who?
Guddu:	He is my dearest friend. My blood.
Lucy:	Tell me his name? And do you remember from Lahore?
Guddu:	Of course I remember you and my attempts to flirt with you. We did not make much headway, much as I wanted to.

...Jassi ... You will know him I am sure.

Lucy:	He has talked about no one else.
Guddu:	Can I see him?
Lucy:	Soon.
Guddu:	But he is here?
Lucy:	He was very badly injured Guddu.
Guddu:	How I wish and pray for him. It was on my persuasion that he came to Europe. I will never pardon myself if he remains a living piece of meat. Oh God. Please help. Give me strength to succeed through this ordeal. Terrible. Terrible.
Lucy:	(*Caressing Guddu profusely knowing how much Guddu valued Jassi.*) Guddu, I am with you to share your grief for Jassi. I have seen many painful events in my life, not least the death of my husband in battle so soon after my wedding. Treat me as the pillar of all the strength that you need. Remain very strong. And I shall be behind you. I have seen you both together in India and I have a deep appreciation of your brotherly life in your culture having lived in India. But these unexpected things do happen in war, though very unfortunate.
Guddu:	You are not aware that he came over here to be with me and at my insistence. He was not afraid to fight. But he was

questioning before he came here, about what the fight is for. True to his self, he fought valiantly. But what for, as he would ask me constantly. And, in this moment of my grief, your intimate manifestation of support is very moving.

Lucy: Guddu, it was the last thing I expected but when I found that both of you are here, I remember how all your officers in India felt so empowered with the results that both of you unceasingly produced in India in the course of your duty, and I was a direct witness to that. I felt something internally as my special responsibility to take care of you both in some ways. I felt a special pleasure in taking care of you both, but specially you.

Guddu: Your support is very useful Lucy. I hear that my dad has heard about me being seriously injured. He is coming to see me here. This will be the first real communication with him. So far, our letters have been very few and far between. The constant battlefield duties have made me forget my family.

Lucy: (*Sobbing*) Guddu, your best friend. Jassi. I am so sorry. He did not survive.

Pammi: (*V/O*) I wept for days. I was surprised that so many tears were available to me. Like a constant stream. I was beyond repair. Or at least I thought that I would never smile again.

Gurnam arrives to see Guddu. Gurnam is able to transmit, carefully, the strong fatherly care and love.

Guddu: Papa, your presence and the love it has brought, has brought all my past memories of my family and Jassi's family. So precious it has been.

Gurnam: I could not sit still ever since I heard of your serious injuries. Jaspreet arranged a flight for me in Maharaja of Patiala's private plane. Where is Jassi?

Guddu:	(*Sobbing*) The war has taken his toll. He did not survive his injuries. But how is it that you heard about my injuries and not of Jassi's?
Gurnam:	This is the least I wanted to hear. Cruel life. Cruel war. But communcations, I suppose, do not follow a chronological sequence. Your news came in. That is it.
Guddu:	I was able to be with him at almost his last breath. But seeing him pass away was very painful. Lucy has written to his father, but you probably left before Jassi's family received the news.
Gurnam:	I came to give you strength. But almost the first news I get is this terrible fate of Jassi. How will Guddi feel? For all her pleadings not to go to fight in a distant land?
Guddu:	And he was so fond of Guddi. Despite seriously being loved by his French hostess Emily. Guddi was his first call. It seemed that he lived for her values.
Gurnam:	Who is this Emily?
Guddu:	A very loving French woman who hosted him for weeks for rest and recreation in France. She was very fond of him. He enjoyed her love and care, but he lived for Guddi.
Gurnam:	War is war, my dear son. Jassi has gone.
Guddu:	Guddi will be upset badly to hear about Jassi. I wish I was with her now.
Gurnam:	So we will need to find a new match for Guddi. We do not know when the war will end. It was not expected to last more than a few months at the beginning. But now, no end is in sight. And the communication with us from our soldiers is very poor. Letters take weeks to come by.
Guddu:	The result of war is uncertainty of life and the timing of the reunion. Think also of Rani.
Gurnam:	I think I will also recommend that Jaspreet should not wait for your return to betroth Rani. Let this be another painful consequence of this war.
Guddu:	Due to the poor communication and battlefield duties, I haven't had time to think much of Rani. I think Rani's future

should not be held a hostage to our duties and this war. So, yes, please find a new match for her. I want to see her flourish and let her not be a hostage to this war. But Dad, how are people feeling over there, about this war?

Gurnam: In elite circles, there is nothing but praise for our men at the battle front. We hear effusive stories. But the undercurrent at the ground level is mixed. News from the loved ones, being able to come in dribs and drabs, does make many people very unhappy. But the counterpart is that many poor families receive regular pay packets every month. They receive it, they pray that their sons come back quickly, but they do not seem to come back any time soon. So some despondency.

Guddu: They allowed you to come here because of the Maharaja. I want you to be with me. For how long can you be here?

Gurnam: I am here only at the behest of the Maharaja. But such visits are not normally permitted. So I will have to go soon.

Guddu: Please do give big hugs to mum, Guddi, Rani and, last but not least, Jaspreet uncle. Tell him I am still alive and I am no different than his son, Jassi.

Gurnam: My sweet light, god willing you will be fine. You are in good spirits and I will report this to everyone back home. At least their soul will be at peace. Bye.

(They part with a soft but deep caress, as Guddu's condition allowed)

SCENE 2

Guddu:	Dad brought a lot of comforting news from back home. I am so happy for Rani and Guddi that Dad has decided to let them flourish and not be a hostage to the vagaries of this war. My parents will not wait for me to come to get them married. I am so happy that they will be settled in life.
Lucy:	Good to hear good news coming especially from home, so far away.
Guddu:	But I wish I could return too. Life is becoming a bit complicated here.
Lucy:	And why is that?
Guddu:	You may already have felt an inkling of that. Your love bug is biting me. I am overwhelmed. With Rani expected to be married, I will have one less problem to handle. But what if your love bug brings us much closer, and closer and closer ...
Lucy:	Guddu ... Guddu ... it's me ... Lucy. What better for a woman than to feel deep and true love.
Guddu:	I can't stop crying.
Lucy:	It's okay.
Guddu:	I wish it had been me.
Lucy:	I don't.
Guddu:	I am responsible for my best friend dying.
Lucy:	Your best friend was killed by the enemy, Guddu, you will never be his enemy.
Guddu:	I have no life now.
Lucy:	That is not true.
Guddu:	I am lost, Lucy.
Lucy:	Let me help you.

Pammi: *(V/O) And she did. In fact, she did more than help me. She changed my life.*

Guddu: I love you, Lucy.

Pammi: *(V/O) There. I said it. This Indian man from Lahore telling his English nurse that he loves her. What was I thinking?*

Lucy: *(With a deep hug)* Oh you have said what I wanted to hear. And I love you too. And I have felt that for some time now. How very fortunate I am to hear this from you. But for me, real love means not ever to betray my love for you and make sure that you keep me drowned in your love.

Guddu: The way you have taken care of us can only be through deep loving and emotional involvement. This was visible and felt by me all the time. But I do not know how to take our love further. Can it be lasting enough to have the power to overcome so many external hurdles? Or external factors will force me just to remain thirsty for you?

Lucy: Most certainly. Deep love with genuine emotions is the most powerful force in life. This can overcome all hurdles. I know that you have the approval issues from your family. And with Rani having married, one less of a barrier for approval for your desires. And let me tell you, we will have the same problems from my family as well. But deep love should prevail over all such hurdles.

Guddu: I look forward to that and I hope I will not have another heart break because of your family. The force of love can and does overcome all unnatural hurdles. The family barriers that overvalue the cultural barriers are in effect unnatural hurdles. Love does not recognize those hurdles. And my in depth love for you is forceful enough to overcome such hurdles.

Lucy: is it really true? Am I living in a dreamworld or a real world? How accident brought us together and sealed our fate. Couples are indeed made in heavens.

A few weeks later

Lucy: Now that you are well enough to move, let us take this opportunity for you to visit my family in London. We will take the
first steps to overcome the hurdles.

Guddu: Welcome. Let this be so. I leave it to you to arrange.

Pammi: *(V/O) London ...*
Guddu

SCENE 3

— — — — — — — — — — — — — — — — —

Guddu and Lucy visit London and meet Lucy's family.

Guddu: Quite disconcerting at some of the things that I had to suffer on the streets of London as a result of not being a white Britisher. Do they have no value for us fighting for them?

Lucy: I did tell you about some of the hurdles that we need to overcome. I will overcome them whether or not my family agrees. But you have now seen, at first hand, at least some of them.

Guddu: Oh yes. I have felt emotions and the insults that were thrown at me. Additionally, I cannot forget the episode at the Ritz.

Lucy: Oh that porter at the Ritz. Scum of the earth. And undoubtedly they are almost a common place in London. It seemed that they have no training to treat all guests fairly and equally. Worse still, you were in uniform and he did not respect even the uniform — the symbol of protecting these very people. I never thought that the feeling against non-English was so strong.

Guddu: What an experience it has been in London. With all this hate and non-acceptance, how do you think you will be able to live with me for the rest of our lives if we were to marry.

Lucy: Did I not tell you that love is a great force. These are small hurdles to overcome. We will be together for our lives when we marry. If I have to choose between all these hurdles and Guddu, Guddu is my unmistakeable choice. Make no mistake.

Guddu: It is very heartening and impressive, Lucy, to hear such strong personal values and emotions from you. Previously I only felt them internally. But you have gone through a battle and have come out unscathed. Your feelings for me are now "battle tested" with your family. With all the fights you have had with your brothers, about me, and all the abuses on the streets of London, I can see your force of love for me. But let me also reassure you, that this force is felt very strongly internally with me. It has still not manifested in a battle-tested format, but it will when such an opportunity arises. It is my love for you that has enabled me to ignore all the negatives that I experienced in London. And ignore those experiences without any rancour in my heart. And all this, because of you.

Lucy: We need to move on. And I only pray that the war sees us through.

Guddu: Precisely. And let Jassi's values be our guiding light, once the war is over. I cannot fight the war if I think otherwise.

Lucy: Fellowship in friendship has a force of love of the same strength as between man and woman. Jassi will forever live with us, in our memory. I know of his thoughts very well through Emily. She used to come so regularly to this hospital to visit us and she betrayed the same love for him as I have for you.

Guddu: How beautiful it would have been if we were to have survived all this fight and both couples could have been together.

SCENE 4

Guddu: I am recovered now, thanks in no small part due to you. And it is all the more sweet now that I have found the most beautiful thing on earth – love – and that too with you. I am able to fly so high in my fantasies.

Lucy: I am really honoured and privileged. To be valued by a brave person like you.

Guddu: I have been posted into a safe position. Not that I am afraid to fight at the front. But I will be able to hope and imagine more of you in the new posting - in the reserve cavalry division. Valuing such love is, after all a most noble sentiment. This is what life is ultimately for.

Lucy: Shall I say that this is wonderful news. I love to think of it to be so, and so do I think, but with all humility. I want to make sure that self-interest does not supersede in my duties to other soldiers. But yes. It is indeed a hearty life development between us that will seal our future.

Pammi: *(V/O) My great grandfather's division was disbanded in 1918 and I was discharged from service and it was time to go back home*

Guddu: Lucy, I am fully discharged and about time to make a lifetime commitment to you. Are you ready to move to India with me where we will marry.

Lucy: Marriage in India ? …. With all the colour and celebrations? …….. Not in my dream did this occur to me. I am thrilled at this thought. This is settled. We will marry in India. After all that you have had to go through with my family and even on the streets of London, I want be a beacon for you to set an example that even overwhelming bigotry can be overcome.

Guddu: I want to go back, My family will enjoy a "trophy" in their family. And you will be that "trophy". And in many ways, my family, who brought me up with such love and care, have hopes and ambitions about me. Jassi's family have been shattered by his death, though they are proud that he died in battle. But Guddi too will welcome you as her sister in law albeit being a committed anti imperialist. Her thoughts do not transcend into opposing the white people. And Rani, too, will be with us.

Lucy: And they are right. I too will join them in their endeavours.

Guddu: That is brave of you. So, prepare yourself. Say good bye to your family.

Lucy: Let us make for the immense losses the people over there have suffered as a result of their participation in this distant war for them. I look forward to work diligently with the people over there.

Guddu: But my unbearable disappointment is that I will be without Jassi. His doubts to come over here were so prescient. Not that he worried about his own life. He was beginning to feel that his life for his people and he wanted to serve them. Alas! This remained only a dream for him.

Lucy: We will try to highlight his memory through community activities.

Pammi: *(V/O) But we never did go back. I was never to return to my homeland again. For me India was over.*

SCENE 5

Pammi: (V/O) On 15 April 1919, General Dyer massacred in cold blood unarmed people who had come to a political rally. Guddu wanted to return to India to feel and share the pain of the people in India. Lucy too wanted the same. But she convinced Guddu that London will be a better forum to get redress. There was already a strong Indian diaspora active politically and she could being in her connections in the upper reaches of the establishment to help get some redress.

Guddu: Is this what we fought for the King for?

Lucy: No words can describe this despicable act. For God's sake, the British project themselves to be the beacon of civilized behaviour. This is the most uncivilized behaviour on their part, a brutality that I have not witnessed ever, and I could never imagine that the British could do this. And these protesters were unarmed. Shameful. Barbaric. I just do not have words to describe it.

Guddu: There is no respect for our people. Our battle willingness and worthiness was also treated with abuse in many quarters. We fought the war. Went through a lot of abuse by many British soldiers even though we fought more steadfastly than many of them, and then the abuse that I went through in London. I always held high my commitment to which I had signed up. But this massacre has broken mine and millions of hearts. Love for the British has evaporated as if in a minute, just like a pressurized superheated vapour. The needle of loyalty has turned one hundred and eighty degrees and the British will pay a huge penalty in lost goodwill as a result.

Lucy: The malaise is deeper than just disrespect for the Indians. The lot of the working people in England are also treated in the same way. Did you read *Oliver Twist* by Charles Dickens? And the Poor Law and workhouse system that he described? We can read a lot through the lines in what he has described in his writings. It is the same callous thinking that is in the heads of the likes of General Dyer. But this General Dyer's order cannot be an excuse for this act.

Guddu: Done is done. He will live to see his fellow rulers regret this day. We will seek redress with the same tenacity we fought for the King on the fields of Europe. Just imagine, even an apolitical figure like myself, has also been deeply affected to almost alienness to the British rule. As I said, evaporated like a pressurized superheated vapour.

Lucy: Guddu, you may not like this. But if we want to see effective redress of this despicable massacre, we should be in London and carry out the struggle there. I have good connections at the upper level in Britain. I will make use of them. All my family are not bigoted. And even those who are, they will not be able to cope with such callous cold blooded murders. Only in London the struggle would find a final solution. The struggle in India will lead only to some little political redress here and there. It has set in motion the call for a more localized government run by the Indians. This trend will ultimately end in Indian self-rule, but will it be total freedom? I doubt it. And soon, they will try to make us forget about this. But this act cannot be forgotten. And it should be a permanent record for posterity, not to be forgotten. And we should struggle against it in London.

Guddu: The political struggle that is now building up to a tsunami will achieve what the mutiny in 1857 could not do. It seems to me that Britain will have lost India for good. But I have a problem. If we do not go to India, my mum and dad will miss their grandchildren when they arrive hopefully in the fair skin ... hahaha.

Lucy: Indeed. And I am suggesting firmly to you that we can only hasten this process if we were to remain in London. Our children will miss the grand parental love, for sure. You will make new friends, many of them Indian, already working for freedom for India, there. This is a struggle for which you will have the full support of your family here in India. We will endeavour to achieve our goals effectively and more rapidly.

Guddu: But how do I resolve matters relating to my family relationships. They are too dear for me. I will, in one stroke, shatter all the hopes that my parents have for me, as their only son. And my sister will feel so ignored. Oh! These are awful thoughts. I do not know how to resolve them. At times I feel devastated. I could not provide enough comfort and joy to my parents. This war took the precious time of joy for my parents, away from me. Was this to be my fate?

Lucy: The little time that I had with your parents were truly a period of paradise for me. As you know, I lost my parents when I was young and I missed all the parental love. But the love showered on me by your parents has been nothing short of total bliss for me.

Pammi: *(V/O) But we never did go back after coming back to London. I was never to return to my homeland again. For me India was over.*

2018.

Pammi: And that's what they did. He never did return to India. Imagine that? Never to return home.

Lily: You're doing that now for him.

Pammi: Am I?

Lily: Yes.

ACT 5

SCENE 1

-- -- -- -- -- -- -- -- -- -- -- -- --

V/O Guddu's children and grandchildren and great grandchildren grow up in England, through English institutions. Pammi read PPE at Oxford where he met Lily, who was from a politically active family. Through discussions, wherein Pammi reminisces about his great grandfather, Guddu and Guddu's inseparable friend Jassi, prompted by Lily, decide that something should be done to remember the sacrifices of the Indian soldiers in the First World War.

In the college Common Room

Pammi: Maybe it is my direct linkage that keeps me passionately interested to honour the fighting men from India. But how do we do that? Something subtle, which is enshrined and has a feeling of permanency about it.

Lily: Well, people do remember the soldiers who lost their lives in the first war and armistice day is a vivid reminder of that. But it is true that that narrative of the armistice day has an underlying reference to the British soldiers only.

Pammi: But Indian soldiers' sacrifices are given a short shrift. I want to convert this recognition to something more respectable.

Lily: Well, indeed, it should be an honour on the part of the government to recognise this in a permanent and continuous way. And when this is done, so many Indians, who now feel fully British, and in most cases, are born here, would develop a new sense of honour. Perhaps it is because we read history written by victors. Britain got the victory and the empire to make. The Indians were only tools for them and they complied with their request in all their innocence and admiration of the Crown. Until Jallianwala Bagh. I recently saw a French publication – Dictionary of the First World war, a 1,000-page book. Would you believe that there is not a word on the Indian soldiers in that book?

Pammi: This is exactly what I mean. The half-truths of history by ignoring the events that were the driving dynamics of politics and war.

Lily: Let us keep on thinking. Some great idea will strike us, sooner or later. I think that we may need to develop a concept of partial sovereignty to honour people who brought glory to our nation in the past.

A few days later

Pammi: It's a stain on the British conscience. It surely is. And, of course, during the period from the end of the Second World War, we see the definition and meaning of human rights elevated to the now exalted level and, dare I say, to a desirable level. Even the rulers in India in the entire history of India resorted to violence against their own people, but it was as plunder for the victors. But Jallianwala Bagh was something special. It was callous massacre to subdue a people, crush their freedom of expression, sovereignty and freedom. This is what is so special about Jallianwala Bagh.

Lily: I'm so sorry.

Pammi: It's not your fault.

Lily: I know, but in a way it is.

Pammi: It is certainly not your fault so many generations after the event. And it is certainly not yours as you have a much more enlightened view on humanity, something that did not exist at the time.

Beat.

Lily: I'm really sorry that my countrymen at the time and after did that to the loyal Indian subjects of the crown. To your grandfather's generation. I'm so … so sorry.

Pammi: And my country too. Different ethnicity no doubt.

They hug.

Pammi: According to the Lonely Planet Guide Goa is going to blow
                our minds.

Lily: Good. Let's go.

Beat.

Pammi: I love you.

Lily: Are you just saying that because I said sorry?

Pammi: No, I'm saying it because like all men from this part of the
                world, when I see a beautiful woman I know how important it
                is to tell them exactly how I'm feeling.

Beat.

Lily: Let's go and blow our minds ... But Pammi, we must search
                for Rani's descendants.

Pammi: Wonderful idea. We should try to establish the same type of
                links that Gudduji had with Jassiji

Lily: That would be a true 360 degree circle.

Music. (From Party of Jassi and Guddu)

Pammi: *It's funny.*

Lily: *What?*

Pammi: *India.*

Lily: *In what way?*

Pammi: *It feels like home and I don't even know it.*

Lily: *It's in your blood.*

Pammi: *Is it?*

Lily: *Of course.*

Pammi: *And England?*

Lily: *Also in your blood.*

Pammi: *It's what they always wanted.*

Lily: *Can we go now?*

Pammi: *Yes. Yes we can go now.*

Lily: *I mean, it's been interesting, don't get me wrong, but I was also prom-
                ised Goa and beaches and sun as part of the Indian experience.*

Pammi: *I'm sorry, you're right. Let's go.*

Pause.

Lily:	*What is it?*
Pammi:	(smells the air) *Always in my blood.*
Lily:	*Come on.*

(They leave.

Fade in Indian music.)

End.